UNA HUNA?

What Is This?

PUBLISHED BY INHABIT MEDIA INC.
www.inhabitmedia.com

Inhabit Media Inc. (Iqaluit) P.O. Box 11125, Iqaluit, Nunavut, X0A 1H0
(Toronto) 191 Eglinton Avenue East, Suite 310, Toronto, Ontario, M4P 1K1

Design and layout copyright © 2018 Inhabit Media Inc.
Text copyright © 2018 Susan Aglukark
Illustrations by Amanda Sandland and Danny Christopher © 2018 Inhabit Media Inc.

Editors: Neil Christopher and Kelly Ward
Art director: Danny Christopher

This project was made possible in part by the Government of Canada.

We acknowledge the support of the Canada Council for the Arts for our publishing program.

Printed in Canada

Canada Council   Conseil des Arts
for the Arts   du Canada

Library and Archives Canada Cataloguing in Publication

Aglukark, Susan, author
     Una huna : what is this? / by Susan Aglukark ; illustrated by Amanda
Sandland and Danny Christopher.

ISBN 978-1-77227-226-0 (hardcover)

     I. Sandland, Amanda, illustrator II. Christopher, Danny, illustrator
III. Title.

PS8601.G53U53 2018   jC813'.6   C2018-904974-X

Una Huna?

What Is This?

by Susan Aglukark

illustrated by
Amanda Sandland and Danny Christopher

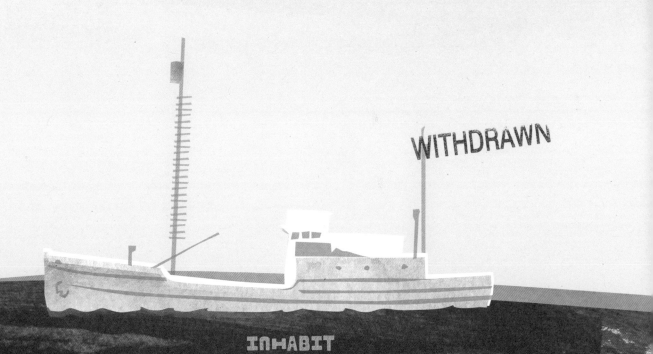

WITHDRAWN

INHABIT
MEDIA

One early summer morning, Ukpik woke before anyone else in the camp. She quietly snuck out of her bed and went outside to play with her new puppy.

Ukpik had yet to name her puppy, and she had snuck out early every morning over the past few days to ponder what she should call him.

Ukpik picked up her puppy and held him in front of her face.

"What shall I call you, Puppy?" Ukpik said. "Hmmm ... *Qimmiq*?" she tried. That word meant *dog*. "Nope, that does not suit you. Maybe *Kuluk*?" Kuluk meant *sweet*, *dear*, or *cute*. Ukpik looked over at her puppy's father, who was a big, strong husky, and laughed. "No, Kuluk is too cute. You won't always be this tiny!"

Suddenly the other huskies started barking in the direction of the water. Ukpik looked out over the water and saw the mast of a ship approaching her camp.

"*Ataata*! Ataata!" Ukpik called to her *father*.

Ataata quickly crawled out of the tent to see what Ukpik was hollering about. A smile appeared on Ataata's face as he saw the ship. He knew the Captain had come back for another season of trading.

"*Tupalikqta! Time to wake up! Makinnaqsijuq! Time to get out of bed!* We have visitors!" Ataata called to the rest of the camp.

Ataata called out instructions, letting everyone know that it was time to prepare for the Captain's arrival. In a matter of minutes, the camp was abuzz with activity as everyone prepared to meet the visitors.

Ataata handed a skin bucket to Ukpik and instructed her to go fill it with water from the stream.

Ukpik took the bucket in one hand and tucked her puppy under her other arm as she walked to the stream to fill the bucket. As she walked, she whispered to her puppy, "What about *Isumataq*?" That name meant *boss*, and it made Ukpik giggle to herself.

When Ukpik returned to camp, a fire had been lit, moss had been gathered to keep the fire going, water was being boiled, and food had been collected and gathered at the fire for breakfast. Ukpik placed her bucket of water by the fire.

She set her puppy down as she sat beside her *anaana*, her *mother*, to eat her breakfast.

"Anaana, I can't think of a name for my puppy," Ukpik said.

"Just eat your breakfast, Ukpik," Anaana said. "We have visitors right now. We'll think of a name later."

Ukpik quietly ate her breakfast, petting her puppy with her free hand. She could not stop herself from thinking about new names.

"Hmmm," Ukpik thought. "How about *Piu, Piu*? Pretty, Pretty? Or *Pinnguaq*? *My Toy*? Or *Qitik*? *Play*?" Ukpik could have thought up names for her puppy all day long!

By early afternoon, the ship had finally landed on the mainland and the camp was busy helping unload. Ukpik's ataata and the Captain were catching up on the past winter's catch and what could be traded for the sealskins and fox furs Ataata had prepared.

"Last summer, I saw you eating with these funny-looking wooden things," Ataata said. "I tried to make some over the winter, but I cannot get big enough pieces of wood to make more. Do you have some to trade?"

"Do you mean forks and knives and spoons?" the Captain asked as he reached into his trunk and pulled out the wooden eating utensils.

"*Ee! Yes!* That is what I mean. I would like some of those for our camp. Maybe a trade?" Ataata asked. The camp had never had eating utensils like this before. The two men came up with trading terms and Ataata was quite happy with his new possessions.

Ukpik stared at the utensils. She was so curious about them! While Ataata was not looking, Ukpik took a set of utensils. Ukpik walked over to the stream with her puppy, where she could watch all the activity in the camp while playing with the new gadgets.

The utensils were wooden, and although the shapes looked familiar, they were still odd by Ukpik's estimation. One was a long stick, thicker at one end and very thin along half its length. It reminded Ukpik of her father's *pana*, his *snow knife*, but it was much smaller. Ukpik decided it must be used for cutting things.

The second piece she could not quite figure out. She poked it into the earth and it picked up a *berry*.

"Hmmm," she said, "look at that, it picked up a *paurngaq*."

Ukpik moved on to look at the third piece. She realized after a while that it was like a little bowl. She dipped it in the stream and, sure enough, the little bowl picked up some water. She put it to her mouth and took a sip. Ukpik was quite excited about these new things, so she grabbed her new toys and her puppy and ran over to show Ataata and Anaana.

"Anaana, Ataata, let me show you something!" Ukpik happily called to her parents.

Ukpik's parents and the Captain all turned toward her. Ukpik picked up the fork and poked it into a patch of berries, saying, "This pokes things!"

Next, Ukpik picked up the knife and looked at her Ataata. "This is like your pana, but smaller."

Then Ukpik picked up the spoon. "This is like a small bowl." Ukpik beamed over her new discoveries. Anaana, Ataata, and the Captain could not help but laugh at her excitement.

"Good for you, Ukpik. You quickly figured out what those are for!" Ataata said through his laughter. "I have an idea," he continued. "Why don't you gather up all the children and show them how to use them?"

19

Ukpik thought about this for a few seconds. "Ee! *Atii*! Yes! *Let's Go*! I would love to do that!"

Ukpik set about gathering all the children and directing them toward the stream. Taking her new responsibility very seriously, she organized the children into a half moon by the stream. She placed the utensils in the middle of them all.

"Okay, everyone, watch and listen," Ukpik said. "These are very important," she continued, gesturing toward the utensils. "I am going to show you how to use them, so you have to pay attention. Be sure to listen. This is very important," Ukpik repeated.

Ukpik decided to start with the knife. "This is the little pana. You can cut things with this, so you have to be very careful with it."

Ukpik's best friend, Qopak, took the knife, and the children took turns studying it. "*Una pilaksisuuq? Does this slice things?*" Qopak said as she cut into a berry. Ukpik smiled at Qopak in agreement.

Ukpik placed the knife back down and picked up the fork. "*Una suurlu kakivak. This looks like a fishing spear,*" Ukpik said. She picked up the kakivak, which they used for spearing fish, as she handed the fork to Qopak. The fork and the kakivak made their way around the group. Each of the kids saw the similarity for themselves.

Ukpik then picked up the spoon. "This is like an *aluut*, a *ladle*, because it scoops water," Ukpik said, as she took the spoon over to the stream and scooped up some water to take a sip, just as she had always done with the ladle used around camp to scoop soup or water. Teaching the other kids about the utensils was a lot of fun.

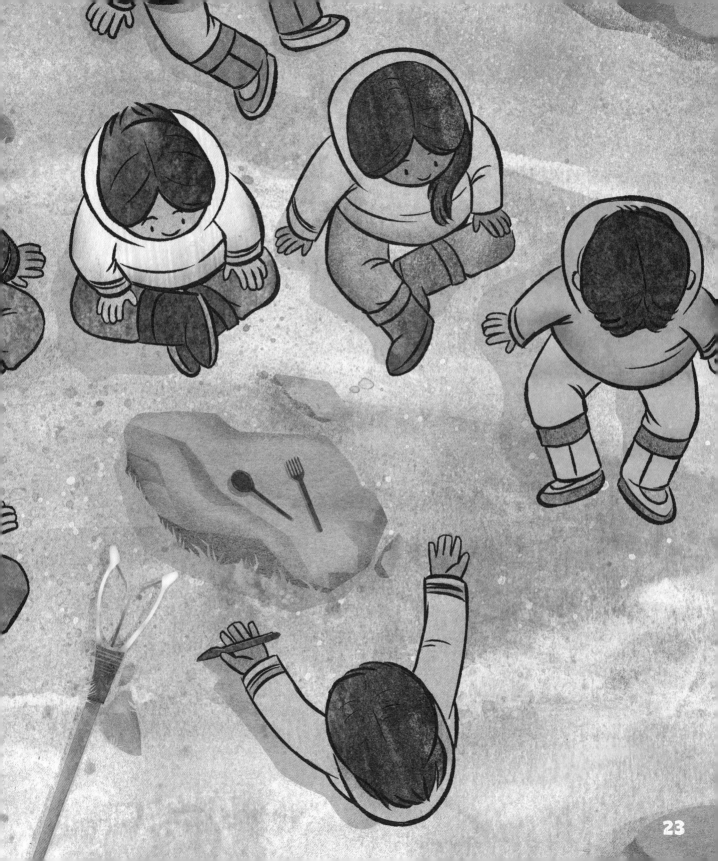

After Ukpik's lesson was over, most of the children made their way back to camp. Ukpik, Qopak, and their friend Anguti stayed behind by the stream.

"I don't think I like these new things very much. Do you guys?" Anguti asked the girls.

"I don't know, Anguti," Qopak responded thoughtfully. "I mean, they don't really bother me, but I can still eat and drink without them. Ukpik, why do you think your Ataata wanted these? Are we going to have to use them all the time now?"

Ukpik thought about this for a few seconds and finally responded, "I don't know, I will have to ask Ataata when I get a chance."

The three headed on back to camp, lost in their thoughts.

Once back at the camp, Ukpik handed her utensils to her *anaanatsiaq*, her *grandmother*, who was cleaning and organizing all the utensils in a bucket.

"Oh, there they are," Ukpik's grandmother said. "I thought we had a set of twelve, one for each family, but I only counted eleven. Thank you, Ukpik."

Rather than Ukpik's usual, cheerful, "You're welcome," Anaanatsiaq noticed her silence.

"What is on your mind, Ukpik?" Anaanatsiaq asked.

"Anaanatsiaq, why do we need these anyway? Are we always going to have to use them? We never needed them before," Ukpik said, looking down at the forks and knives and spoons.

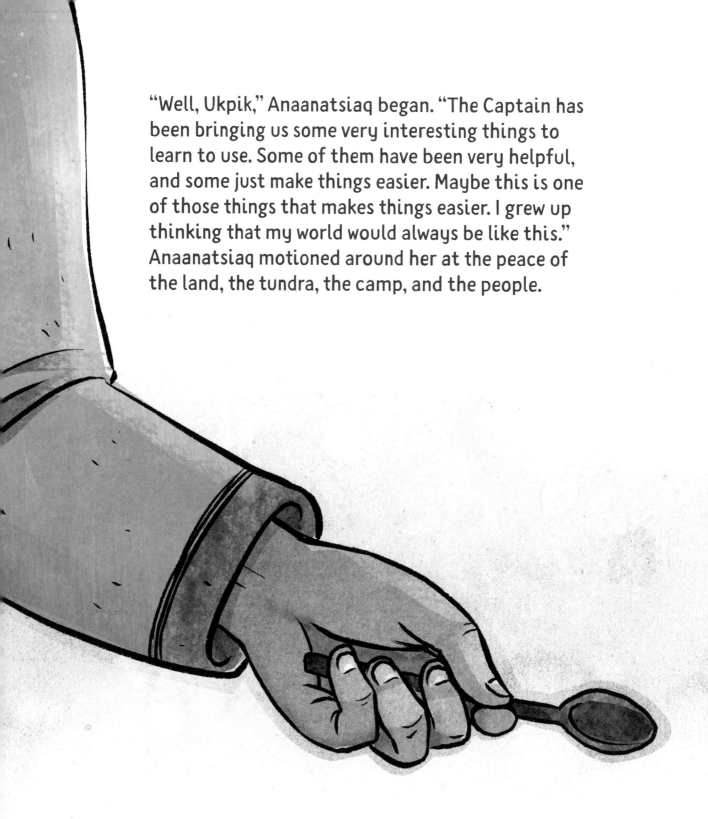

"Well, Ukpik," Anaanatsiaq began. "The Captain has been bringing us some very interesting things to learn to use. Some of them have been very helpful, and some just make things easier. Maybe this is one of those things that makes things easier. I grew up thinking that my world would always be like this." Anaanatsiaq motioned around her at the peace of the land, the tundra, the camp, and the people.

"But when the Captain first arrived, I saw for the first time that all of this is a gift, and slowly we are sharing it with the Captain's people. And in turn, slowly his people are sharing their ways with us."

Anaanatsiaq reached down and placed a spoon in Ukpik's hand.

"Now, every time you spoon up some soup, you will think of the aluut. Some things happen that can never be unlearned or forgotten. The Captain arrives, and every time he returns we are anxious for new things. But he brings us only what he can, so we learn only what he gives us. Our minds and hearts want to learn more, and we are impatient. There is nothing we can do about this, so we get even more anxious. This is what you are feeling. You have so many questions, and we don't even have the words yet to ask with. That is our challenge, Ukpik, to understand what is in that other world a little bit at a time. Even if our world will not stay the same, our camp and our family will always be here to learn about these new things together."

Ukpik leaned into her grandmother, spoon in hand, and looked out at the water's edge where Ataata and the Captain were drinking tea and talking.

Her puppy scampered up to her and jumped into her lap. As she looked down at his little fluffy face, Ukpik whispered, "I think I'll call you *Uummat.*"

That word meant *heart* or *loved one.* As Ukpik sat watching the people and the camp that she loved so much, it seemed like a perfect fit.

GLOSSARY

aluut (ah-loot): A ladle for liquids

anaana (a-naa-na): Mother

anaanatsiaq (a-naa-nat-chee-aq): Grandmother

Anguti (an-goo-tee): Name, also means man

ataata (a-taa-ta): Father

atii (ah-tee): Let's do it, let's go

ee (ee): Yes

isumataq (i-sooh-mah-taq): Boss

kakivak (kah-kee-vak): A fishing spear

kuluk (koo-look): Sweet one, cute one, dear one

makinnaqsijuq (mah-kin-naq-si-juq): Time to get out of bed

pana (pah-na): A long snow knife

paurngaq (pah-ooh-ngaq): A berry

pilaksisuuq (pi-luck-si-sooq): To cut through items

pinnguaq (ping-ooh-aq): A toy

piu (pee-ooh): Pretty or precious, often used as a term of endearment

qimmiq (qim-miq): A dog

qitik (qi-tik): To play

Qopak (qoo-pak): Name

suurlu (suur-loo): As if (as if it were any other)

tupalikqta (too-pah-liq-ta): Time to wake up

Ukpik (ook-pik): Name, also means owl

una (ooh-na): This (person or item)

uummat (ooh-maht): Heart or my heart

SUSAN AGLUKARK is Canada's first Inuk artist to win a Juno. She has also won a Governor General's Performing Arts Award for lifetime artistic achievement and she is an officer of the Order of Canada. Susan holds several honorary doctorate degrees and has held command performances. During a career that has spanned more than twenty-five years, Susan's journey as a singer-songwriter has led her to reflect on who she is, where she comes from, and the importance of discovery— discovery of history, culture, and self. This time of reflection, writing, and songwriting has Susan coming back to one area of profound knowing: Inuit are an extraordinary people deeply grounded in a culture forged by their ancestors. Her children's book, *Una Huna? What Is This?*, and her upcoming album are inspired by these reflections and cultural connections. Visit susanaglukark.com for more information.

AMANDA SANDLAND is an illustrator living in the Toronto area. She studied illustration at Seneca College, eventually specializing in comic arts and character design. When not drawing, she can be found studying, designing characters, creating costumes and replica props, or burying her nose in a comic.

DANNY CHRISTOPHER is an illustrator who has travelled throughout the Canadian Arctic as an instructor for Nunavut Arctic College. He is the illustrator of *The Legend of the Fog*, *A Children's Guide to Arctic Birds*, and *Animals Illustrated: Polar Bear*. His work on *The Legend of the Fog* was nominated for the Amelia Frances Howard-Gibbon Illustration Award. He lives in Toronto with his wife, four children, and a little bulldog.

INHABIT
MEDIA

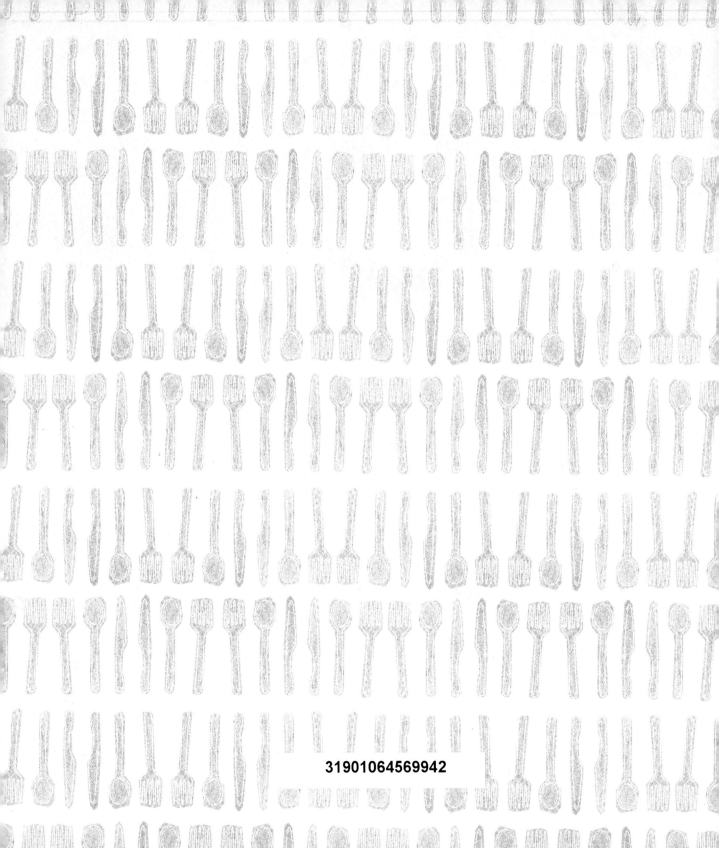

31901064569942